Dear Parents:

Congratulations! Your child is taking the first steps on an exciting journey. The destination? Independent reading!

STEP INTO READING® will help your child get there. The program offers five steps to reading success. Each step includes fun stories and colorful art or photographs. In addition to original fiction and books with favorite characters, there are Step into Reading Non-Fiction Readers, Phonics Readers and Boxed Sets, Sticker Readers, and Comic Readers—a complete literacy program with something to interest every child.

Learning to Read, Step by Step!

Ready to Read   Preschool–Kindergarten
• big type and easy words • rhyme and rhythm • picture clues
For children who know the alphabet and are eager to begin reading.

Reading with Help   Preschool–Grade 1
• basic vocabulary • short sentences • simple stories
For children who recognize familiar words and sound out new words with help.

Reading on Your Own   Grades 1–3
• engaging characters • easy-to-follow plots • popular topics
For children who are ready to read on their own.

Reading Paragraphs   Grades 2–3
• challenging vocabulary • short paragraphs • exciting stories
For newly independent readers who read simple sentences with confidence.

Ready for Chapters   Grades 2–4
• chapters • longer paragraphs • full-color art
For children who want to take the plunge into chapter books but still like colorful pictures.

STEP INTO READING® is designed to give every child a successful reading experience. The grade levels are only guides; children will progress through the steps at their own speed, developing confidence in their reading.

Remember, a lifetime love of reading starts with a single step!

Visit us on the Web!
rhcbooks.com

Educators and librarians, for a variety of teaching tools, visit us at RHTeachersLibrarians.com

ISBN 978-0-593-81366-9 (trade) — ISBN 978-0-593-81367-6 (lib. bdg.)
ISBN 978-0-593-90004-8 (ebook)

Printed in the United States of America

10 9 8 7 6 5 4 3 2 1

THE GARFIELD MOVIE

One Lucky Cat!

by Nicole Johnson
based on the screenplay by Paul A. Kaplan
& Mark Torgove and David Reynolds

Random House 🏠 New York

This is Garfield.

He is a kitten.

He is all alone . . .

and hungry!

This is Jon.

He is lonely.

He sees Garfield.

Jon loves Garfield.

Garfield loves Jon, too!

Jon brings Garfield

to live with him.

This is Odie.

Odie lives with Jon
and Garfield!

Odie loves Garfield.
He helps Garfield with
anything he needs,
like making a midnight
snack!

Garfield likes
to eat.

His favorite food
is lasagna.
He also likes
pizza, sandwiches,
ice cream, and more!

Garfield has a big,
comfy chair.
It even plays music!

He hates Mondays.
Garfield thinks that
bad things happen
on Mondays—
like going to the vet!

This is Vic.
He is Garfield's dad.

Vic loves
Garfield.

Vic and Garfield do not always get along.

But Vic will always
be there for Garfield.
They are a family!

This is Jinx.

Jinx is a mean cat.

She is fluffy and
very cranky!

She does not like Vic.

Jinx scares Vic!

Roland and Nolan
are Jinx's sneaky
helpers.

They follow Garfield
everywhere!

This is Otto the bull
and Ethel the cow.
They are Garfield's
newest friends!

Garfield loves all his
friends and family.

He is one
lucky cat.